"Check out this cool present from my dad," said Francine.

"Is it some kind of supersonic sweeper?" asked Binky.

"No," said Buster. "It's for finding alien spaceships!"

"I'll show you what it does at the beach," said Francine.

When they got to the beach,
Francine pressed the ON button.

"Stand back," she said.

It made a strange crackling sound—then a few beeps.

"Look!" said Francine, pulling a bottle cap out of the sand.
"It's a metal detector. You use it to find buried treasure."

"That's not treasure," sniffed Buster.

"I bet there's lots of neat stuff hidden here," said Arthur.
"We just have to find it."

They combed the beach for two hours.

"Wow!" said Buster. "One old fish hook, six bottle caps, a thimble, and a broken pair of sunglasses."

"This isn't worth anything," said Binky.

"I don't understand it," said Francine. "The instruction book says you can find gold and silver and lots of other valuable stuff."

"Maybe we're doing it wrong," said Arthur.

"I'll bet the good stuff is buried way down below..." she said.
"We better start digging."

Everyone got down on their knees.

"Keep going. You have to dig at least five more feet," Francine said. "I read that in a book about buried treasure."

"We don't have any shovels!" said Binky.

"Keep digging," said Francine.

Francine climbed into the deep hole and turned on the detector. It clicked and crackled, then stopped.

"Shh!" whispered Francine. "I think I'm getting something..."

The detector started to make a loud beeping sound.

"I found something!" cried Francine.

"It's a pirate's doubloon!" Francine shouted.

"Wrong," said Binky.

"It's a gold ring!" she tried again.

"Negative," said Buster.

"A lump of gold?" she said.

"I don't think so," said Arthur.

"Well, what is it?" asked Francine.

"It's some kind of coin," Arthur said.

"It looks like a penny," said Buster.

"It has a princess on it," said Binky.

"That's not a princess, silly," said Francine. "That's the Statue of Liberty."

"Well, she is wearing a crown," replied Binky.

"This is really old," said Francine. "Aren't old coins worth a lot of money sometimes?"

"I don't know," said Arthur. "But I know who *will.*"

"The Ultimate Guide to Coin Collecting should tell us," said the Brain. He studied a page...then the penny... then another page.

"What is it?" asked Francine.

"The numbers and letters are hard to read," said the Brain.

He came to a picture and gasped.

"Wow! I don't believe it," he said.

"What is it?" cried Francine.

"This is one of the rarest coins in the Western Hemisphere: the Lucky Lady Liberty penny!"

"I'm rich!" said Francine.

"It's only worth about ten-thousand dollars," said the Brain.

"Ten-thousand dollars!" cried Francine, dancing around the room. She took the penny and put it in her pocket.

"I dug for hours," said Buster.

"I'm the one who saw the crown," said Binky.

"I found the coin in the guide," added Brain. "You really should share with all of us."

"It's my metal detector, so it belongs to me," Francine said.

"No fair!" they all cried.

The next day Francine made a long list of all the things she'd buy with the ten-thousand dollars.

Muffy helped.

"And don't forget a few presents for your best friend," said Muffy. "If that were my coin, I'd put it in a bank vault. It's very valuable!"

After Muffy left, Francine decided to put the coin away in a special hiding place.

But later, when Francine went to hide
the penny, she couldn't find it.

She looked under the bed. She looked in
her closet. She looked in every drawer.

"It's gone!" cried Francine.

Francine went to the playground.

"How's your Lady Liberty penny?" asked Binky.

"I lost it," said Francine.

"How could you lose it?" asked Buster.

"I looked everywhere," said Francine. "But it's gone."

"That's too bad," said Muffy.

"Maybe we could help you find it," said Arthur.

"Share the work," said Binky.

"Share the reward!" said Buster.

Francine agreed, "*If* we find *it*."

Arthur and his friends turned Francine's room upside-down.

"It's gone," sighed Buster. "Let's go."

"Wait," said Arthur. He turned on the metal detector.

"I'm getting a reading," he said, following a beeping sound.

The closer he got to Muffy, the louder it beeped.

"I don't have it!" cried Muffy.

But when she lifted her foot, there it was on the bottom of her shoe stuck to a wad of gum.

"I found it!" Arthur said. "I mean, *we* found it."

"Found what?" asked Francine's dad.

"The Lucky Lady Liberty penny," explained Francine.
"It's worth ten-thousand dollars!"

Mr. Frensky examined it closely. "I hate to tell you, but this is just a plain old Liberty penny."

"The book said the 1902 coin was worth ten-thousand dollars," said the Brain.

"This coin is from 1932," said Mr. Frensky. "The three is almost worn away. It's worth about ten dollars. Sorry."

"Figures," said Francine.

"Easy come, easy go," said the Brain.

"So, what are you going do with the ten dollars, Francine?" asked Buster.

"I know exactly what to do with it," said Francine. "Where's the phone?"

Francine passed around the pizza she had ordered.

"Dig in!" she said.

"No more digging! Please!" said Binky.